Sonny and Little Cloud

Carol Wilson Covington

ISBN 978-1-64258-607-7 (paperback)
ISBN 978-1-64258-606-0 (digital)

Christian Faith Publishing, Inc.
832 Park Avenue
Meadville, PA 16335
www.christianfaithpublishing.com

Printed in the United States of America

Buckets of love and sunshine to Kate, Jackson, Caitlyn, Hadley, Drew, Colin, and Nicholas, and also to my biggest encourager and supporter, Olin.

A special thanks to my eight year old "Junior editor", Jackson, who suggested I illustrate and publish this story from "my mouth".

Sonny did not like storms at all! He really, really, *really* didn't like storms. When he hears that one was coming—and especially during the storm—he would hide under his blanket, under his bed, or under the kitchen table. Sometimes his stomach felt jumpy. Sometimes his hands shook or his head hurt. He just didn't like storms until one special day!

That stormy day Sonny was under the kitchen table with his blanket covering him. Finally, the storm grew quieter, and Sonny peeked one eye out from under his blanket to look out the window. His mouth dropped open! On the other side of the window was a small storm cloud looking back at him. The little cloud had a huge grin on his face.

"Whatcha playing under that table?" the little storm cloud asked.

"I'm not playing. I'm hiding, and I'm scared," said Sonny.

"Whatcha scared of?" asked Little Cloud with a smile.

"You!" was Sonny's reply.

"Me? Why are you afraid of me?" Little Cloud said as his smile slid from his face.

Sonny was quick to answer. "I don't like thunder, I don't like lightning, I don't like big wind, and I don't like much rain. I just really don't like storms. *Any* storms!"

Little Cloud looked very sad. "Thunder? You don't like thunder? Why thunder is just me playing.

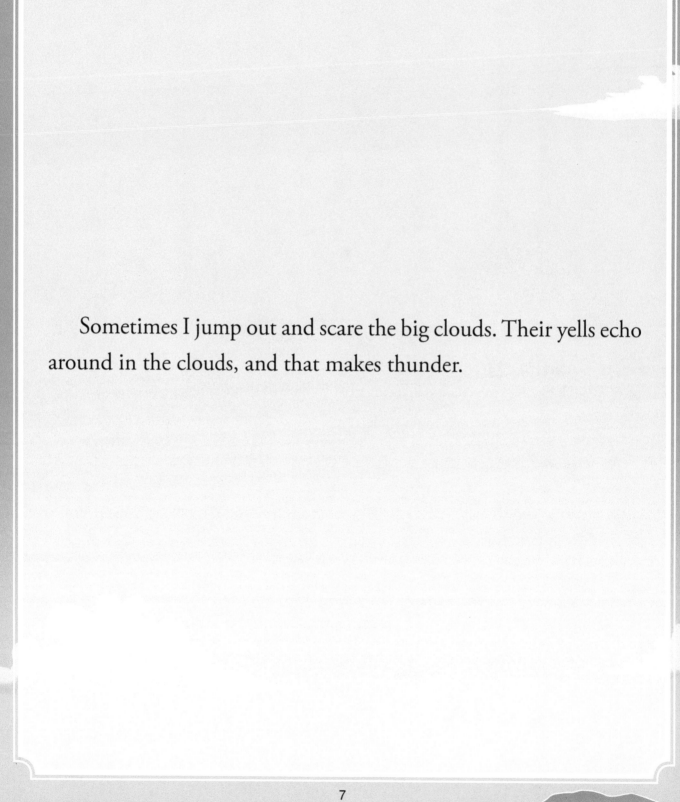

Sometimes I jump out and scare the big clouds. Their yells echo around in the clouds, and that makes thunder.

Sometimes I go bowling. The long thunder is just my bowling ball rolling down the alley. Sometimes I just laugh really, really loud. Or sometimes I get the hiccups. Those are the short thunder sounds you hear. Thunder won't hurt you."

Sonny thought about this and then added, "Maybe I'm not really afraid of thunder. I just wish it wasn't so loud."

Little Cloud thought for only a minute. "You shouldn't be playing outside when there is lightning though. It could hurt you really badly. Sometimes I play hide-and-seek behind the big clouds. I can pop out over there one minute," he said, pointing toward the trees, "and over there the next."

This time he pointed toward the empty lot. "I scare the big clouds that way. They yell and get angry at me. Then you see the lightning if they really get angry," Little Cloud said with a sheepish grin. "Then the lightning can go all the way to the ground. I kinda like that though. It adds nitrogen to the earth that helps trees and other plants grow. Just remember to head indoors when you see lightning."

"Okay," Sonny said. "I promise not to play outdoors if it's lightning. Now, Little Cloud, what's so good about wind?"

Little Cloud started to smile again. "Betcha you have watched the trees and flowers dance when the wind races through them, haven't you? That's the only time they get to shake their leaves and really have fun. Wind spreads seeds and pollen around to make new plants and make your earth beautiful. It can also run giant windmills to make energy for your home. I like wind!" Little Cloud announced.

Sonny was starting to understand all Little Cloud had said. He took off his blanket and crawled out from under the kitchen table. As he moved closer to the window, he said, "Now, Little Cloud, tell me about rain."

"Yipee!" shouted Little Cloud. "Rain is my favorite! My very, very favorite." Then he began to laugh. "Have you ever watched a pig play in his mudhole after a good rain?"

"No," answered Sonny. "But I have played in a few mudholes myself."

They were both laughing now.

Little Cloud began, "Every living thing on earth depends on water to survive. You drink it. Animals and birds that live outside drink it and take baths in it. Flowers, trees, grass, fields, and gardens need it to grow and live. Water fills lakes and streams for you to play in. It also cleans streets in cities and towns. It even cools the temperature of our planet earth."

"Have you ever smelled the sweet, clean smell after a rain on a hot summer day? Oh yeah, and have you ever seen a beautiful rainbow? Gotta have water to see that. Yep, rain is my favorite."

Just then a clap of thunder rang across the clouds.

"Gotta go," Little Cloud said. "That's my dad calling me. It's time for us to move on."

At the same time a gust of wind started to push Little Cloud away from the window.

Before he had drifted too far, Sonny shouted to Little Cloud, "Come back again, Little Cloud. Wonderful things happen because of you. And because of you, I'm not scared anymore. I don't have to hide from thunder, wind, or rain. But I promise I won't play outside when it's lightning. Please come again."

About the Author

Carol is the mother of three and a grandmother of seven. She and her husband live in western Kentucky. Carol and Olin are now retired and spend much of their time working with their church, volunteering in the community, traveling and visiting the grandchildren who live in Ohio, Georgia, and Kentucky. She served twenty-one years on the local school board. Some of her favorite days are the ones she dresses as Mother Goose and visits local schools and day care centers to try to bring Mother Goose to life and instill the love of reading to the children. When a child asks her a question such as "Did Jack have to go to the hospital?" or "Did you see Humpty Dumpty's yellow insides?" she knows she has triggered their imagination.

Six years ago, when grandson, Colin, started asking her to "tell me a story from your mouth, Gram," she realized she might have a story or two that other children might enjoy also.

CPSIA information can be obtained
at www.ICGtesting.com
Printed in the USA
LVHW071028030219
606202LV00050B/1832/P

9 781642 586077